Little Mouse's Rescue

Ariane Chottin
Adapted by Patricia Jensen
Illustrations by Malgorzata Dzierzawska

Reader's Digest Kids
Pleasantville, N.Y.— Montreal

Squeaky was a little mouse who lived on a farm. She slept in a cozy nest high off the ground. She loved to race through the great stalks of wheat and play hide-and-seek with her friends. But most of all, she loved to sneak into the farmer's kitchen and nibble on the crumbs she found there. This was a very dangerous thing to do—because two big, mean tomcats lived in the house.

"I'm not afraid of those cats," the foolish little mouse always said.

One day, Squeaky called down to her friends, Max and Rosie, "Wake up, sleepyheads! We're going on an adventure!"

It didn't take long for Squeaky to convince her friends to join her. The little mice sneaked under the back door of the farmer's house. Then they quickly climbed up to the kitchen counters, where they found all kinds of wonderful foods.

Squeaky looked at Max and Rosie with a great big smile. "Dig in!" she squealed.

After the mice had eaten their fill, they scurried safely out of the house.

That night, Max and Rosie slept soundly, but Squeaky tossed and turned. She couldn't stop thinking about all the delicious food in the farmer's kitchen. "Perhaps if I had just a small nibble of something, I would be able to fall asleep," she murmured.

So the foolish mouse hopped down from
her nest and dashed back into the house. She
crept past the sleeping cats and headed straight
for the kitchen.

Squeaky climbed onto the kitchen counter. "Wow!" she gasped. "More treats!"

She quickly began stuffing herself. She ate bread crusts, cheese, nuts, fruit, and even some cake. Finally, Squeaky stopped eating. She could not squeeze in another bite.

"Mmmm," the little mouse said sleepily, "that was the best snack I've ever had." She yawned and stretched. "Maybe I should lie down for a couple of minutes before I head back home."

In an instant, Squeaky was sound asleep.

Rosie soon discovered that Squeaky was not in her nest. "I know where she's gone," said Rosie. "To the kitchen!"

Max was still sleeping, so Rosie found a few other friends, and together they searched the kitchen high and low. They looked in the teapot and in the drawers. Finally, Rosie spotted Squeaky.

"There she is!" Rosie called. "In the flour sack!"

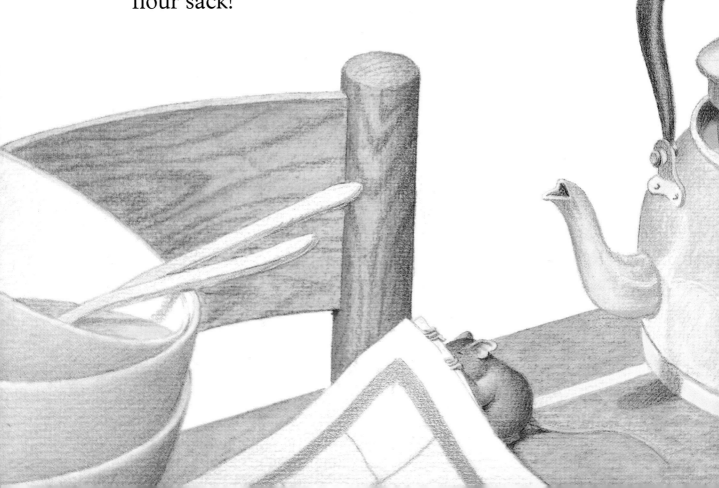

The little mice tried to wake Squeaky, but she was too full and too sleepy. The only response they got was a loud snore.

"We'll have to carry her," Rosie decided. "But be very quiet. We don't want to wake up those awful cats!"

The mice lifted their fat friend and began creeping out of the house, past the two big cats. Suddenly, one cat raised its head and opened an eye.

"Oh, no!" gasped Rosie.

Then the big orange cat slowly closed its eye and went back to sleep.

"That was a close one!" whispered Rosie.

The mice carried Squeaky safely outside
and headed toward her nest. On the way, they
met Max. The mice put Squeaky down. They
wanted to see if she could walk by herself, but
she could not even open her eyes.

"She'd better be grateful for what we're doing," grumbled Rosie as she pushed Squeaky along. "If we hadn't gone after her, she would be the cats' breakfast."

The mice tried carrying Squeaky again.

"She's just too heavy," complained Rosie. "I need to stop and rest."

"Not yet," whispered Max. "What if the cats wake up and come after us? What if an owl sees us standing around? Look, it's not much farther to Squeaky's nest."

"You're right," sighed Rosie. "Let's keep going."

After much huffing and puffing, the mice finally made it home safe and sound.

The next morning, Squeaky listened as Max and Rosie told her about their adventure.

Squeaky couldn't believe how foolish she had been. "How can I ever thank you for rescuing me?" she asked.

"Just promise you'll never do that again!" said Max.

"We wouldn't want to lose you over some silly treats," added Rosie.

"I promise," said Squeaky. "Besides, the best treat is having good friends like you."

The mouse belongs to the rodent family, which includes squirrels, chipmunks, groundhogs, gerbils, and hamsters.

Mice gnaw on almost anything they find. They will damage books, furniture, clothing, and electrical wires. They will even gnaw on pieces of soap!

Mice can hear well, but they have poor eyesight. Their long whiskers help them feel their way around in the dark.